Dedicated to Zoe and Jonah,
my inspiration.

I love when my parents plan a big BBQ
with all of our family and friends!

The best part is going to the butcher shop on Main Street to get our meat for the BBQ.

The butchers are so friendly!
They even give me a slice of cheese
(or bologna)!

The butchers are very very careful
when using their knives.

Chicken

Mommy likes to say that
the butchers are artists.

Hamburgers, steaks, ribs,
sausages, chicken, lamb chops...
so many yummy choices!!

The butchers will cut the steaks for us exactly how we like it.

We always like to buy bacon and eggs before paying the cashier.

On the drive home, I am so excited to watch Daddy cook on the grill...

We all eat and laugh and tell stories
and laugh some more.

When we are done eating,
my tummy is usually really really full.

I will fall asleep so quickly because of our busy day and my full belly.

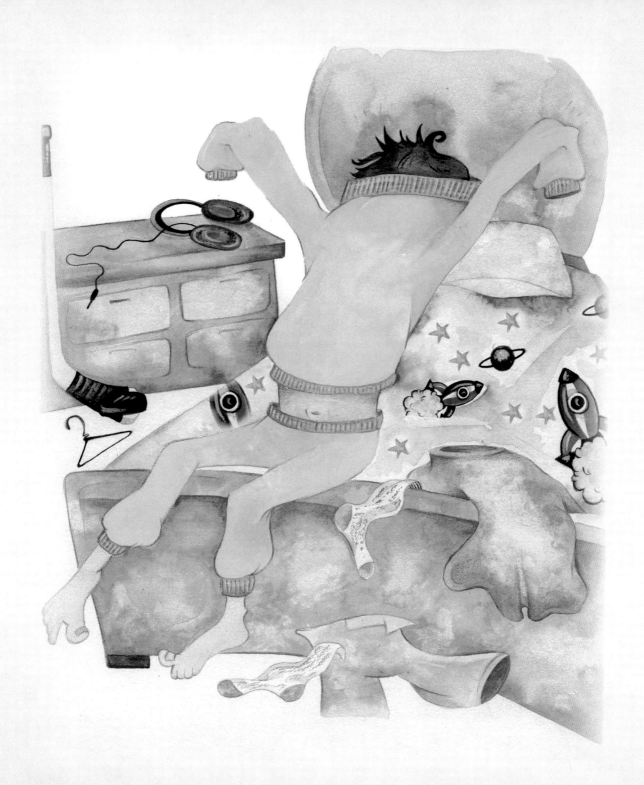

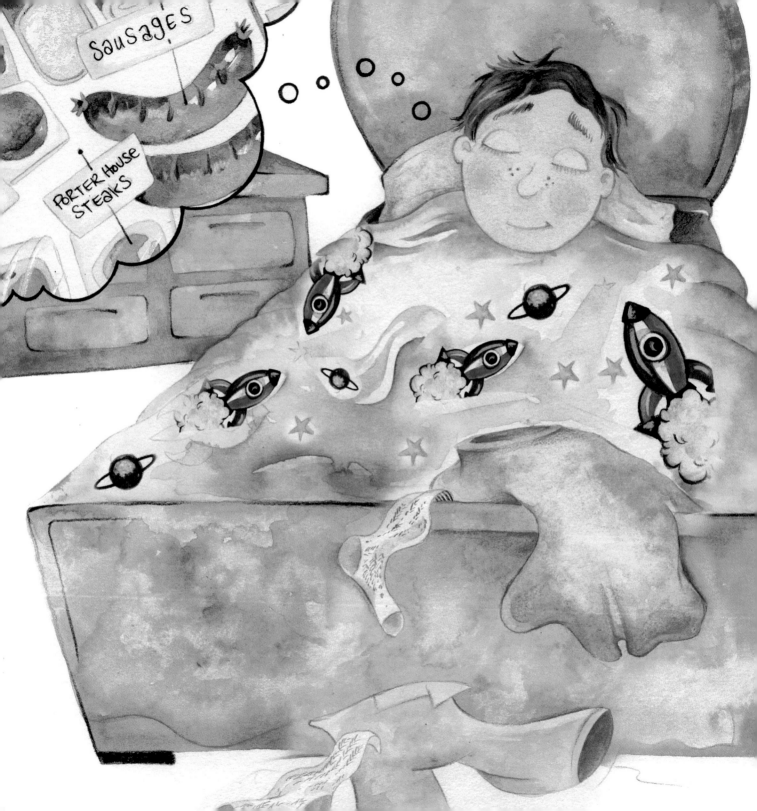

I dream about our next family BBQ
and seeing the friendly butchers
on Main Street again...

Made in the USA
Middletown, DE
17 March 2023

26981775R00024